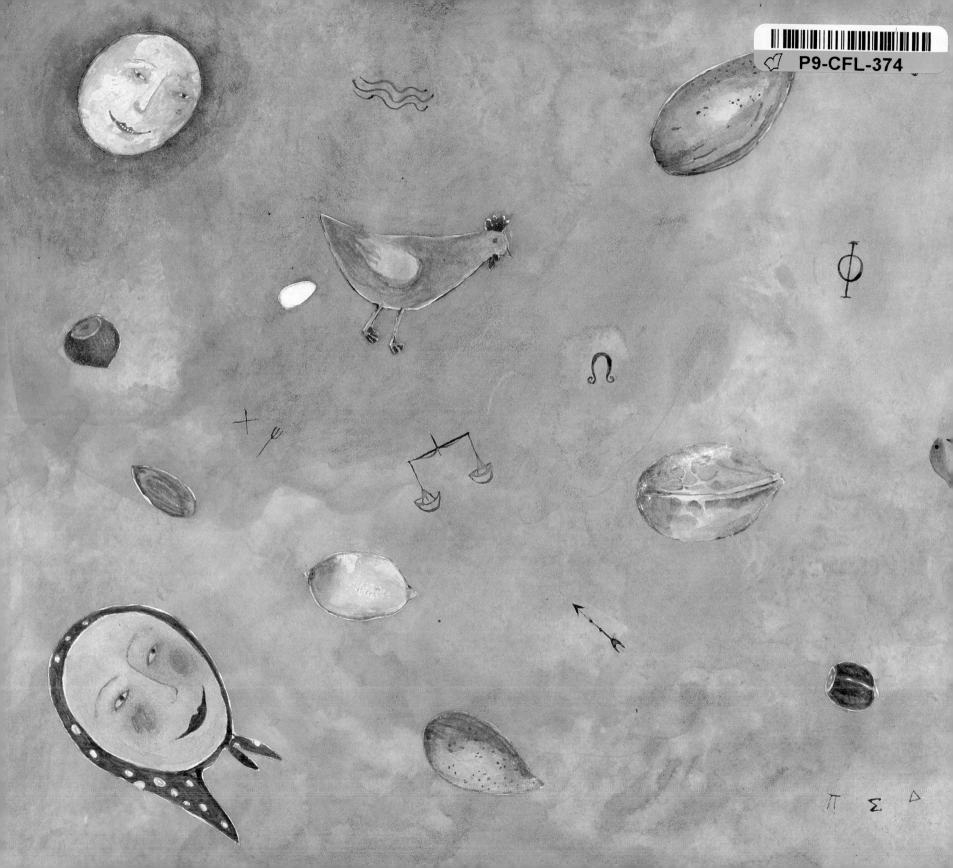

P9-CFL-374

Mr. Semolina-Semolinus

A Greek Folktale

Retold by Anthony L. Manna and Christodoula Mitakidou

Illustrated by Giselle Potter

THE BRYANT LIBRARY
2 PAPER MILL ROAD
ROSLYN, N.Y. 11576-2193

AN ANNE SCHWARTZ BOOK

ATHENEUM BOOKS FOR YOUNG READERS

3 1490 00315 0295

For all the special folks in Greece who taught us how to trust the wisdom of the word. Efharisto!
—A. L. M & C. M.

To Mama and Christian
—G. P.

Grateful acknowledgment is offered to Melpomeni Kanatsouli,
Greek folklorist at Aristotle University, Thessaloniki, Greece.

A Note About This Story

Tales that tell of inanimate objects brought to life appear in many countries. The theme of the person whose desire for love is so powerful that he or she can make even a doll or statue come alive is a favorite among storytellers in the eastern Mediterranean countries of Italy, Greece, and Turkey. In Greece alone, there are some forty versions. Most common are ones like *Mr. Semolina-Semolinus,* in which the person who longs for a companion uses sugar and other common cooking ingredients like semolina, a wheat extract, to make an ideal human being.

Areti, the name given to the heroine in *Mr. Semolina-Semolinus,* is the Greek word for virtue.

Atheneum Books for Young Readers
An imprint of Simon & Schuster Children's Publishing Division
1230 Avenue of the Americas
New York, New York 10020
Text copyright © 1997 by Anthony L. Manna and Christodoula Mitakidou
Illustrations copyright © 1997 by Giselle Potter
All rights reserved including the right of reproduction in whole or
in part in any form.
Book design by Angela Carlino
The text of this book is set in Bernhard Modern.
The illustrations are rendered in colored ink and colored pencil.
First Edition
Printed in the United States of America
10 9 8 7 6 5 4 3 2 1

Library of Congress Cataloging-in-Publication Data
Manna, Anthony L.
Mr. Semolina-Semolinus : a Greek folktale / retold by Anthony L. Manna and
Christodoula Mitakidou ; illustrated by Giselle Potter.—1st ed.
p. cm.
"An Anne Schwartz book."
Summary: Areti, a Greek princess, makes a man fit for her to love from almonds,
sugar, and semolina, but when he is stolen away by a jealous queen, Areti searches
the world for him.
ISBN 0-689-81093-8
[1. Folktales—Greece.] I. Mitakidou, Christodoula. II. Potter, Giselle, ill. III. Title.
PZ8.1.M2978Mr   1997
398.2'09495'01—dc20
[E]   96-1924

One time in a time, in Greece, there lived a king who had a daughter. Her
name was Areti, and she had many suitors. But she wanted none of them because she
liked none of them. So one day she made up her mind to make a man of her own.

She took three pounds of almonds, three pounds of sugar, and three pounds of semolina. She pounded the almonds, added the sugar and semolina, and kneaded it all together. And she made herself a man!

For forty days and forty nights she prayed to God.

On the fortieth day God brought the man to life. People called him Mr. Semolina-Semolinus. He was five times beautiful and ten times kind, and his name became known the wide world over.

As it happened, a queen from a kingdom far away heard of the beautiful Mr. Semolina-Semolinus and desired to have him for her own. She built a golden galley with golden oars, and set sail for where he lived. When she arrived, she ordered her sailors, "Whoever stands out five times above all others for his beauty and ten times for his kindness, seize him!"

"Yes, queen," they answered, and off they went.

Hearing that a magnificent golden galley had arrived, all the townsfolk from far and near went to the docks. So did Mr. Semolina-Semolinus. As soon as the sailors saw him, they knew who he was. They grabbed him at once, and into the galley he went.

Meanwhile, Areti waited for Mr. Semolina-Semolinus to return from the docks. She waited . . . and waited. . . . But nothing. She asked one person, she asked another and another. And then, she heard what had happened!

What could she do?
What *did* she do?
The princess ordered three pairs of sturdy iron shoes made and set off in search of the beautiful Mr. Semolina-Semolinus, of course. She traveled on and traveled on, she took roads, she left roads, until she wore out the first pair of iron shoes.

Areti now looked out at the end of the world, and before her stood the mother of the Moon.

"Good day, dear mother," Areti said.

"Welcome, my child. How did you ever happen to this land?" she replied.

"My destiny brought me. Did you by chance meet a man who is five times beautiful and ten times kind? His name is Mr. Semolina-Semolinus."

"But where? I have never even heard such a name," said the mother of the Moon. "Wait for my son to come at daybreak. He travels the wide world over and may know."

When the Moon returned that dawn, his mother said, "My son, this girl begs you to tell her if you have seen Mr. Semolina-Semolinus."

"No, I have not, my girl," replied the Moon. "But go ask the Sun. He too is a world traveler and may know."

Before the princess left, they gave her an almond and told her, "When in need, break it."

Again, the princess traveled on and traveled on, she took roads, she left roads, until she wore out the second pair of iron shoes. Before her stood a woman so dazzling, Areti had to shield her eyes. It was the mother of the Sun. She had not seen Mr. Semolina-Semolinus either. "Wait for my son to come at nightfall," she suggested.

When the Sun returned home, the princess knelt before him and asked, "My Sun, my World Wanderer, have you by chance seen Mr. Semolina-Semolinus?"

"No, I have not. But go to the Stars that are many," he replied. "Perhaps one of them has seen him."

Before the princess left, they gave her a walnut.

"When in need, break it," they told her.

Areti traveled on and traveled on, she took roads, she left roads, until she wore out the third pair of iron shoes. Before her stood the mother of the Stars.

No, this mother had not seen Mr. Semolina-Semolinus. "Why don't you wait for my children to come home," she said. "You can ask them."

So when the Stars returned that morning, Areti asked, "Have you seen Mr. Semolina-Semolinus anywhere?"

"No, we have not," the Stars replied.

But then the smallest Star cried out, "I saw him!"

"Oh! Where?" Areti cried.

"Where the seven white houses meet the seven black inns. There lies a kingdom ruled by a queen who keeps him and guards him so that no one can take him away."

Before the princess left, the small Star showed her the way, gave her a hazelnut, and said, "When in need, break it."

Yet again, the princess traveled on and traveled on, she took roads and she left roads, till her bare feet were cracked and sore. Finally, she came to the exact spot the Star had described—and there she set eyes on the beautiful, the kind Mr. Semolina-Semolinus.

Now how could she get him away from the queen?

Days passed . . . the princess in her ragged clothes did not approach . . . and still did not approach. . . . At last she remembered the nuts! *Maybe these can help,* she hoped, and stepped forward.

Areti went directly to the servants and begged, "Please let me stay here for a few nights. I do not mind sleeping in the goose house."

The servants asked the queen, who replied, "Why not? Put her there."

So they did.

But just in case, that night the queen gave Mr. Semolina-Semolinus a drink, and this drink had sleep in it. As soon as he'd tasted it, he fell to the ground, snoring. The servants picked him up and brought him to the beggar in exchange for the wheel.

Once the servants had gone, the princess started talking to Mr. Semolina-Semolinus. "Why don't you wake up? Aren't I the one who made you . . . who pounded the almonds, added the sugar and semolina, and kneaded it all . . . who traveled to the end of the world to find you? And you won't even talk to me?"

On and on she pleaded, the whole night long. But would he wake up? No!

In the morning, the servants took Mr. Semolina-Semolinus back to the queen. She gave him another drink and he woke immediately.

Next the princess cracked the walnut and out came a silver hen with silver chicks.

When the queen heard about them, she said to her servants, "Run! Tell the beggar to give us this hen and her chicks. What does she need them for? If she tells you she wants Mr. Semolina-Semolinus, fine. What can happen?"

All passed as before. But when Areti was alone with Mr. Semolina-Semolinus, would he wake up? No!

Finally, the princess cracked the hazelnut and out came a carnation plant with bronze carnations.

When the queen heard about it, of course she wanted it. She said, "If that girl asks for Mr. Semolina-Semolinus, you know what to do."

The servants went and told the princess.

Now next to the goose house there lived a tailor who sewed at night. Night after night, he'd had to listen to the beggar girl's pleadings, and he wanted an end to it. So he went to Mr. Semolina-Semolinus and said, "Many pardons, your majesty, but I must ask you a question."

"Ask away," said Mr. Semolina-Semolinus.

"Where do you sleep at night?"

"At home, dear sir. Where else would I sleep?"

"Master Semolina-Semolinus, I have not been able to sew a stitch for two nights because of that beggar you have in the goose house. All she does all night long is cry, 'Mr. Semolina-Semolinus, why don't you wake up? I traveled to the end of the world to find you, and you will not even talk to me!'"

Ah! thought Mr. Semolina-Semolinus, and his heart skipped a beat, for he felt sure that this was his beloved come to rescue him. But all he said was, "I'll see what can be done."

That night the queen gave Mr. Semolina-Semolinus the sleep drink, but he only pretended to swallow it and fall asleep. Immediately the servants picked him up, carried him to the princess, and took the carnation plant with the bronze carnations.

As soon as the servants had left, Areti began to pour out her grief.

"Hush now, my own sweet love. Cry no more!" begged Mr. Semolina-Semolinus, opening his eyes.

To the princess he now appeared ten times beautiful and twenty times kind, for that is the way love is. "I have missed you so," she said.

Then together they mounted Mr. Semolina-Semolinus's horse and rode off.

In the morning when the servants went to get Mr. Semolina-Semolinus, they found not a trace of him! They ran crying to the queen—who started crying also. But what could she do?

"I can make myself a man," she said at last. She ordered her servants to crack many almonds, mix them with sugar and semolina, and shape them into a man. But as she began to pray for him to come alive, only curses came out of her mouth. Forty days later, the man spoiled and had to be thrown away.

Meanwhile, the princess and Mr. Semolina-Semolinus had sailed home to Greece, where they lived blissfully but no better.

I was there, I should know.

THE BRYANT LIBRARY

3 1490 00315 0295

J
398.
09495

Manna, Anthony L.
    Mr.
Semolina-Semo-
    linus

1500   7/97

WITHDRAWN
OM THE COLLECTION OF
HE BRYANT LIBRARY